THE PERFECT FAMILY

by

EMMA MATEO

TABLE OF CONTENTS

PROLOGUE

The Collins family had it all. Henry Collins had a very successful architecture and real estate business, a beautiful mansion he inherited from his father, a wonderful wife named Madeline, and three amazing children. The twins were the oldest, Crystal being born an hour before Xavier, and their younger brother Adrian.

The Collins family had fame, wealth, a functional family, and all the love and support one could ask for. They had everything to gain, but also everything to lose. Now, with Crystal's husband Gabriel running for mayor, Xavier and his husband James trying to adopt a child from China, and Adrian trying to stay off drugs as he was raising his 8-year-old little girl Ava, it wasn't a good time for the police to investigate them for murders that happened when the twins were only 18.

It wasn't a good time for Crystal's various affairs to come to light, or for Gabriel to have an accident because of drunk driving. It wasn't a good time for Madeline to have a stroke, or for Henry to decide to sell his incredibly successful company. It isn't a good time for a strange woman named Clara Chavez to claim she is Henry's daughter.

The seemingly perfect All-American family is falling apart, and everybody's watching.

CHAPTER 1

Henry and Madeline

Henry woke up in a bad mood, as per usual.

"Breakfast!" Henry grumbled, snapping at the unfortunate maid who happened to be bringing him his food.

"Henry!"

Madeline snapped, glaring at him from the other side of the table,

"Where are your manners?"

Henry grumbled again, eating whatever his fork landed on.

"Stupid woman." He muttered, chewing loudly.

"Honestly, you could never tell you came from money, the way you eat! Close your mouth!"

Madeline said, her voice like the edge of a knife.

"Make me!"

Henry almost shouted, sending a glare her way that would make hell freeze over. Breakfast continued this way, until one of them finished with their meal. Then the couple went to their shared room and got dressed smartly for the day. Madeline donned a pantsuit, pinning her white blonde hair up and away from her face.

She left promptly at 8:30 every morning to go help design buildings in the family company, Collins Architecture. Henry dressed in a suit, usually navy blue or black, putting just enough gel in his now grey hair to keep it in place. He left at about 9:00 every morning. Sometimes he was a little earlier, sometimes he was a little later.

No matter what time he got into the office, within the next hour he was talking to somebody. If it wasn't investors, then it was clients. Henry just hoped that through all of the talking and sales that he had to do throughout the day, he wouldn't have to deal with Madeline. At 6:00 in the evening, both Henry and Madeline got off work. They drove themselves to their mansion, and ate around the large dining table with all of their family.

The entire Collins family ate at the old Collins mansion every night, each of them talking about what they did during the day. For Ava, the only grandchild, it was her time to shine. Ava got to brag about everything she had done that day, and if nobody else would listen, then Grandma and Grandpa would hang off her every word.

Adrian may or may not show up for the family dinners. When he wasn't strung out, then he would be in the corner of the table, next to his daughter. The children, now adults and married, at the other end of the table would talk about whatever they had going on in their lives. When dinner was done, everyone would disperse and go back to their respective houses.

Henry and Madeline let the fake smiles and fake happy relationship they put on for dinner fade away, and they were back to screaming at each other. Of course, they made sure that Adrian and Ava were in their wing of the giant mansion before they did anything that could be taken the wrong way. Henry and Madeline were very aware of the fact that they had to at act happy and not let their children or grandchild see them as anything less than perfect.

Especially not with Crystal's husband Gabriel running for mayor. The Collins family was already in the spotlight because of the fact they were from old money, and they continued to make millions a year, but with the added pressure of a political campaign on their shoulders, the media would skin Henry and Madeline alive if there was trouble in paradise.

Henry and Madeline were in bed by 10:30, both of them on opposite edges of the bed. The next morning, they would wake up and start the process over again, maybe throwing an interview or two in there as the election drew closer and closer.

CHAPTER 2

Crystal and Gabriel

Crystal wakes up to an empty bed, pounding headache, and ear splitting ringing blasting from her phone. She groaned and answered her phone, swearing to herself that she would change the ringtone.

"Yes?" She asked, holding her pounding head in one hand and her phone in the other.

"Crystal, did you get up okay? You had a rough night last night."

Gabriel's voice comes from the phone, and Crystal groans. His voice was too sickly sweet for her to deal with today.

"Yes babe. I had a rough night, but I got up like normal."

Crystal lies through her teeth, the constant pounding in her head making it hard for her to concentrate.

"I left some aspirin and water beside the bed so-"

Crystal stops listening to Gabriel, zoning out and thinking about the man she was going to meet after she stopped talking to her husband.

"Babe? Crystal? Cryssy?" Gabriel asks from the other end, snapping Crystal from her reprieve.

"Yes Gabe?" She says, paying Gabriel as much attention as she could through the pain in her head.

"I'll talk to you later Cryssy. Bye. Love you." Gabriel says, disconnecting the call before Crystal could say anything.

Crystal doesn't mind though, throwing herself back onto the bed and taking the aspirin on the bedside table. She laid there, thinking about her life and how she screwed everything up when she rushed into marrying Gabriel.

She was stupid to marry somebody she had no interest in. An hour later, Crystal is dressed and out the door. She was on her way to meet the man of the day, Jack or Jackson or something like that. She did the same thing every day she could, going out and meeting a random man to have sex with before rushing home to take a shower, dry her hair, redo her makeup, and dress nicely so she could greet Gabriel at the door with a chaste kiss before he went to their bedroom to change so they could go to the family dinner together.

Rarely did Crystal ask questions about how Gabriel's day had gone, though Gabriel asked about Crystal's day every evening when they were making the drive to the Collins family mansion. Small talk was never a strong point for Crystal, so Gabriel just assumed that this was the way she was normally.

Crystal wanted nothing more than to tell Gabriel all about what she was doing behind his back, but she knew the consequences of doing so. Gabriel may be a loving person who wanted to make as many people happy as he could, but he would never forgive her for breaking his heart.

Crystal was painfully aware of how clueless her husband was, thinking she loved him even half as much as he loved her. And she knew if Gabriel divorced her, she wouldn't see a cent of the family fortune.

Crystal was really stupid to have married Gabriel, but she did it so she would be able to live her life without worrying about her actions working their way back up to the ears of her parents.

Crystal knew she never loved Gabriel, and probably never would, but she put on a fake smile and kissed her husband so nobody knew what she did when she was alone. Crystal just hoped that she wouldn't have to please or appease her husband in any other ways than looking like the perfect housewife who supports her husband in all of his endeavors, even when they keep him away from the house for long periods of time. Dinner, as always, went nicely.

Adrian pushed food around his plate, Ava bragged about even the littlest thing she did that day, Madeline hung off her every word, Xavier and James whispered to each other about different things as they commented on the conversations going on around them, Gabriel attempted to talk to Henry as they ate, and Crystal talked to Xavier and James as she ate small amounts.

The perfect family scene. Adrian was the first to rise from the table and go to his room, leaving Ava in the care of her grandparents, aunt, and uncles. Xavier and James were next to leave, smiling and laughing as they told everybody around the table that they would see them the next night, swinging their joined hands as they walked out the door.

Crystal envied her twin's happiness. She envied how in love he was. She wanted what he had. Crystal and Gabriel were the last of the people leaving to actually leave, thanking Henry and Madeline for hosting dinner like always. Without much thought, Crystal kissed her mother and father on their cheeks and said good bye, hoping she had avoided suspicion for yet another day.

Later that night, when Crystal and Gabriel were in bed, Crystal lay awake long after Gabriel kissed her goodnight and rolled over, snoring within a few minutes. Crystal let the tears roll down her cheeks in the darkness of the bedroom. She didn't want this life; she didn't want what was handed to her.

Crystal also didn't want Gabriel to suffer because of her actions. No, she could never love him, but that doesn't mean she doesn't care for him. They had been married for three years now, and spending that much time with another person who was always nice made it hard not to form attachments.

CHAPTER 3

Xavier and James

Xavier woke up with James curled around him, snoring in his ear. He couldn't help but smile at James, even if he was pretty sure the snoring would make him deaf.

"James. Babe, wake up." Xavier said, trying to wiggle is way out of James' grasp.

"James!" Xavier sighs, smiling despite the fact he really had to go to the bathroom and James was not letting him go. The snoring had stopped though, so Xavier knew James was awake.

"I don't want to let go." James mumbled, holding Xavier tighter.

"Yes honey, I love you too, but I really need to use the bathroom. I don't think you would appreciate being peed on." Xavier says, again trying to wiggle out of James' grasp.

James lets him go this time, laughing when Xavier accidentally falls out of the bed.

"I'll go get breakfast started. Pancakes sound good?" James asks, smiling sleepily at Xavier.

"Yeah, sounds good to me." Xavier replies, making his way to the bathroom finally.

Half an hour later, James and Xavier are seated at the breakfast bar in their apartment, laughing with each other as they eat blueberry pancakes and fresh cut peaches.

"Come on! There is no way she was flirting with you!" Xavier says, snickering.

"Oh shut up! I'm hot and you know it!" James defends, sticking out his tongue.

Xavier pecks James, laughing as they finish their breakfast. Three hours later, Xavier and James are walking hand in hand through a local mall, making their way to the adoption agency they had read about online. A woman smiled at them when they walked in.

"Xavier and James I assume?" She asked with a smile.

When they nodded, she continued.

"I'm Ashly Redens and I will be taking care of you today. If you will just fill out the rest of these forms, telling us the gender of the child you wish to adopt, the country you wish to adopt from, and other such questions about more personal information most adopters are unwilling to provide online."

Ashly explains, leading them to a small room with a desk and a couple chairs, handing them papers and pens before closing the door as she walks out of the room. Half an hour later, Ashly is back in the room and checking their credentials, smiling widely when everything checks out.

"Aright then gentlemen, I have a couple matches for you from China. You said that any gender would be fine, but you wanted a child from China under the age of three. We have a nice woman set to have a baby in three months who is putting the child up for adoption because of pressure from her family, and a child that just turned four that you could go pick up next week."

Ashly says, looking at them as she reads the information from on the screen.

"Could we have a couple minutes to discuss our options?" James asks, sending a look towards Xavier. Ashly nods and makes her way out the door, telling them that she will be with them soon. When Ashly returns to the room, Xavier and James inform her that they wish to adopt the child that is not yet born.

"We think that it would be a better fit for us, no matter the gender of the child. If we could go with that option, that would be great." James says, Xavier nodding along.

Ashly then smiles and puts in their request, telling them they would have to have multiple other meetings before anything could be confirmed. Xavier and James then make their way back to the car so they could go to dinner at Xavier's parents' house before heading back home.

They couldn't help but hope they would be able to adopt a lovely child from China without having to wait years in order to do so.

At dinner, Xavier and James told the family what they had done, and how they hoped to be able to bring home a baby sometime soon.

The family wished them well, though Ava, realizing that she would no longer be the only grandchild, was upset by the news. All in all, when the lights were turned off that night and Xavier thought about how the day had gone and what was going to happen, he was elated that something so wonderful was happening.

Now all he had to do was find a way to get out from under his family, and make sure they didn't hurt the baby he and James hoped to receive.

CHAPTER 4

Adrian and Ava

Adrian groaned when Ava bound into his room, screaming about something.

"Ava, what do you want now?" Adrian asked, not even bothering to open his eyes to look at his child.

"It's noon daddy. I'm hungry and nobody else is here." Ava says, jumping up onto her father's bed.

She was all to use to this weekend routine. Ava could get up whenever she wanted to and her grandma would have left food on the counter for her to eat, but there was nothing she could do for lunch. Being only 8, Ava couldn't very well make herself something for lunch. She couldn't reach anything in the kitchen, and didn't know how to make anything yet.

"Daddy, please get out of bed. I'm hungry." Ava says, making her small hands into fists and hitting her father in the chest.

"I'm getting up now darling. Just go wait in the kitchen for me to get there. I'll be there soon, I promise." Adrian says, finally cracking open his eyes.

"Okay. I'm coming back if you don't get up." Ava replies, jumping down from the bed and running toward the kitchen.

An hour later, Adrian has made Ava something to eat for lunch, and made sure she had enough snacks for the rest of the day. Adrian loved his daughter to death, but he loved getting high more. So out he went to get his next fix.

Out into the world without making sure his daughter would be okay until somebody was there to watch her. Without a backward glance, Adrian was out the door to meet up with his dealer. All he could think about was his next high, his next window of feeling like nothing would hurt him. Heroin, Adrian's drug of choice, made everything better for him for a few hours.

As long as he kept shooting up, nothing could go wrong. As long as the needle pierced his skin, as long as the honey liquid enters his veins, everything in the world will right itself.

Even though the crashing fall of withdrawal is worse than anything Adrian could ever imagine, he still chased the next high. In order to fly you must fall, after all. In the long hours between Ava's father leaving and her grandparents coming home from their jobs, Ava tried not to cause trouble. Normally she would eat whatever Adrian made for her, then watch something on TV while she was waiting for other people to arrive.

Ava wouldn't tell her grandparents how long she had been there; wouldn't tell them she knew what Adrian was doing. No matter how often he left Ava alone in the giant mansion she called home, Ava still loved her father. She still kept her promise not to tell anyone about how Adrian left her alone.

Ava was a smart little girl, and she knew her father was doing something he wasn't supposed to, but she didn't know exactly what. Still, Ava didn't tell anyone in her family. Even her favorite uncle, James, wasn't privy to the information.

Ava just wanted her father to love her and keep her safe like her friend's fathers did. Ava wanted her father to see her and not something else outside. Ava just wanted to be loved by the one person she loved more than anyone else.

Her father was the one person who never seemed to be completely interested in what Ava had to say, and as much as Ava disliked it, that made her hurt. No, Ava would never be able to tell you why it made her sad her father wouldn't pay attention to her, but she knew that it hurt. She knew that's not what you should do to your child.

Adrian, on the other hand, thought that he was giving Ava as much attention as any parent should. He thought letting her do whatever she wanted to was good for her. Adrian also saw that this system made it simple for him to be able to leave her for hours at a time without any regrets or remorse. As much as Adrian loved Ava, he undoubtedly loved getting high more.

More than anything else, Ava craved love and affection from her father, and Adrian craved the release of a high. Adrian knew how to get what he wanted. Ava had no idea how to get what she wanted. Dinner was always an event.

Ava tried as hard as she could to make everybody pay as much attention to her as possible. Adrian always pushes the food around his plate, eating just enough nobody decides to ask questions. Ava is loud and proud, wanting the entire table to hang off her words.

Most of the time she was the sole attention holder of Henry and Madeline, Adrian didn't pay much attention to anything as his thoughts were consumed with other things, Crystal and Gabriel almost always were talking to Xavier and James instead of paying any attention to the people at the other end of the table. Every night she remembered, Ava would run up to her uncles, screaming their names as they picked her up and tossed her around in the air.

Once every few weeks Ava would even insist on sitting between James and Xavier, talking to them endlessly as Crystal threw looks to her twin that clearly said "Your problem."

After dinner, Madeline would make sure Ava got to bed on time, brushed her teeth, and didn't ask too many questions about her father not being there. When Ava went to bed at 8:30, Adrian was almost never still at the house.

Normally he would leave before dinner was even completely finished, heading out to chase his next high. If he was still at the house, he was in his room using his stash. Adrian locked the door to try to protect Ava, but his family still knew what he was doing.

When Adrian finally fell asleep sometime around two in the morning, he never woke up before noon. When the sun finally made it's rude awakening, Adrian would be out and searching once again for his next fix.

CHAPTER 5

The Trouble Begins

Ava is woken up by somebody ringing the doorbell again and again. She checks the alarm clock beside her bed, and seeing that her grandparents would still be home she ran downstairs.

"Grandma! Grandpa! Who's at the door?" Ava yelled, almost tripping when she was met with a tall lady with shockingly red hair.

"Grandma? Who's she?" She asked, confused with the situation.

Ava could tell something was wrong because this mystery woman had rang the doorbell, and nobody ever did that. Also because Henry had a very scared and shocked face, and Ava had never in her short life seen her grandfather shocked or scared by anything. Quickly, before Ava could see or hear much more, Madeline was ushering her out the door and telling Ava how they would take a day and go to the mall.

"What about school Grandma? Won't I get in trouble?"

Ava, despite being excited about going out with Grandma, who always bought her anything she wanted, was worried about what would happen to her if she missed school and wasn't sick.

"It's okay to skip a day here and there. We need some time together, alright Ava? I haven't been seeing enough of my favorite grandchild lately!" Madeline jokes as she tells one of the maids to make them breakfast.

"Is that okay with you Ava?" She asks, sitting at the breakfast bar.

"Alright Grandma!" Ava replies, forgetting all about school as fresh chocolate chip pancakes are placed under her nose.

Madeline and Ava leave around the same time Madeline usually heads to the office, taking one of the "big" cars and heading for a nearby small town that mostly consisted of mom and pops shops and small diners.

The main attraction of the town was a truck stop half a mile away. In the meantime, Crystal woke up not hungover for the first time in a long time. She got up, got dressed, took a long shower, and shot a text to the guy of the day.

An hour later, whichever guy she happened to text was sitting next to her on the couch. The situation would stay innocent for no more than the next two or three minutes before a heavy make out session began.

Of course, in the thrall of cheating with an attractive guy in the house that she had bought with her husband, Crystal failed to notice the door open. She failed to notice the voice of her husband panicking at the door, but Crystal did notice when Gabriel dropped some sort of glass.

Crystal did notice when glass went everywhere and Gabriel started yelling for the man to leave his house.

Crystal's eyes welled up with tears as she stood up and adjusted her clothing.

"Gabriel I can explain! I kn-" She starts, fully ready to try and explain away her horrendous actions.

"Stop!" Gabriel cuts her off with an unusually gruff shout.

"We have to get to your parents' house immediately. Your father needs all the support he can get right now. We will be talking later Crystal."

Gabriel steps around the glass on the floor and takes Crystal by the wrist as he leads her out of the house.

"Baby! Gabe! Gabriel! Please try to unders-" Crystal tries again, struggling against his forceful grip.

"I just explained that we will talk about this later. Right now you need to put on a smile and act like you love me. It shouldn't be hard." Gabriel hisses, once again cutting Crystal off.

"I do love you Gabriel." Crystal says, trying to reason with Gabriel. She's never seen him so upset before, and it's scaring her.

"Our baby can't be from a broken home." Crystal is crying and emotional and she forgets she hasn't told Gabriel the news yet.

"Our baby? What do you mean our baby?" Gabriel is immediately softer and his grip lessens. Crystal gulps. She can't help it; she really didn't mean to tell Gabriel yet.

"I-I'm pregnant Gabe." Crystal looks down at her feet and rubs the wrist Gabriel let go.

"We will talk about all of this later, I swear. We do have to get to your parents' house though."

Gabriel seems so conflicted Crystal doesn't push the issue and gets into the car without further question. When Crystal and Gabriel walk into the dining room at Crystal's parents' house, they are met with the sight of a woman with bright red hair staring at their father as he looks more stressed than either of them had ever seen him.

"Yes! Please take a seat! Xavier and James should be here soon. Adrian has disappeared again." Henry says as he looks up at his only daughter and her husband.

Crystal and Gabriel don't hesitate to take seats across from Henry and the strange woman. Xavier and James walk in just moments after Crystal and Gabriel sit down, both of them taking seats on the same side of the table.

"What do you need to talk to us about Dad?" Xavier asks, eyeing the women in the seat next to his father.

"Yeah! And who's that woman?" Crystal asks, eyeing the red head with disdain.

"I'm sorry to tell you all this under these circumstances." Henry begins.

"Your mother is out with Ava, don't give me that look Xavier." Henry shoots a look toward his son. "This woman-"

"Clara Chavez" The woman interjects. Henry gives a quick nod of affirmation.

"As I was saying, this woman claims to be my child. I have never once cheated on Madeline, so this claim is unfounded and a crazy accusation." Henry folds his hands together on the table.

"However, this would also be a nightmare for us in terms of press."

"What are you saying Henry?" Gabriel asks, looking uncomfortably at Clara. The other people seated on that side of the table made similar remarks.

"He means that he wants you to help him decide if he should pay me off or not. I will go to the press if Henry decides not to pay me." Clara speaks up, locking eyes with each of them in turn.

"You can't do that! It's blackmail!" James exclaims, shaking his head in disbelief. Clara gives a smile so chilling Crystal actually shivers.

Gabriel and Xavier, who are on either side of her, both reach out and grab one of her hands.

"I know exactly what it is. And you have my terms." Clara stands up and throws her red hair over her shoulder.

"You can expect to see more of me. I will get my money. You abandoned my mother as soon as you found out about me, so now I want my penance." Clara walks calmly out of the house, not even sparing the magnificent house a second glance.

CHAPTER 6

The Police Come A Knockin'

After Clara leaves, none of the people at the table could make the move to leave. Crystal was in tears, but Gabriel didn't lift even a finger to help her. Gabriel was actually mad this time, and a few tears from Crystal wasn't changing that.

Xavier was similarly upset, despite the fact he disliked his family and harbored a certain amount of resentment towards them. He was leaning heavily on James, and it didn't look like he was moving anytime soon.

Henry sat where he had before, his face like stone. None of the people sitting around the table could tell what he was thinking or what he would end up doing. They all knew it would be no problem to just pay Clara the money she was asking for, but they also knew that isn't the way Henry works. They sat there, not talking to each other or moving to get up from the table.

Eventually, Ava ran through the room, heading up to her room to drop off the things her grandmother had bought for her.

"Daddy!" She screams as she takes the large stairs as quickly as she can.

"Daddy! I got some stuff f-" Ava's childish voice fades as she goes up the stairs.

Madeline followed behind her only grandchild, smiling absently at her innocent actions. Then she turns her attention to most of the rest of her family sitting at the dining room table.

"It's not dinner time already, is it?" She asks, taking the seat Clara occupied before. Crystal looks up at her mother, pushing her long white blonde hair from her face.

"Mom." She says, looking conflicted.

"Can- can I talk to you? In the other room? Alone?" Crystal finally says, taking a hair tie from her wrist and throwing her hair into a messy bun.

"Of course dear. I'll have the cooks start with dinner before we go. I guess I didn't realize how late it was getting." Madeline answers, giving her only daughter a soft smile.

As Crystal and Madeline exit the room, Ava bursts into it, giggling in the way only an innocent child can.

"Uncle Xavier! Uncle James! Come see what Grandma got me! Come on! Come on! Come on!" Ava almost screeches, pulling on both of their hands. The couple shares a secret smile before complying, letting their niece lead them up the stairs and to her room. They both loved Ava dearly, and enjoyed how much she wanted them to be involved with her.

Gabriel was fine being second string to Xavier and James, as he didn't particularly like children in the first place. He didn't want to have children at all, and the news of Crystal being pregnant really upset him.

Almost more so than the news of her cheating did. Gabriel and Henry were left alone at the table, looking at each other carefully.

"Why are you acting so cold towards my daughter?" Henry asks, studying Gabriel carefully. Gabriel swallows hard, looking at the ground instead of his father in law.

"I'm not acting differently." Gabriel says eventually, attempting to smile.

"You are acting differently and you know it. Tell me why or I will ask Crystal. You know damn well she can't lie for the life of her." Henry threatens, glaring at Gabriel.

"We've just had a fight, that's all. I don't want children, she does. I'm always faithful, she's apparently not." Gabriel's voice turns to acid as he speaks, betraying the emotion he had been trying to hide. Henry starts to laugh, the loud sound echoing through the large room. Gabriel looks perplexed, not understanding at all why Henry was laughing like that.

"You really think Madeline and I have been faithful this whole time?" Henry asks, calming himself down.

"You need to understand that we play by a different set of rules than you do Gabe." The way Henry says Gabe like he's trying not to barf makes Gabriel shiver. He doesn't like the way the familiar nickname sounds coming from Henry.

Gabriel makes a move to say something about the unfairness of the situation, but Henry cuts him off.

"You will not ruin my daughter's reputation by divorcing her, are we clear?" Henry offers up a chilling smile, his voice void of any emotion. Gabriel can't help but gulp as he nods, not quite understanding the situation he was placed in.

Madeline and Crystal return to the room, and Henry smiles and offers up a laugh, Gabriel still looking altogether uncomfortable.

"What did you two talk about when we were gone?" Crystal asks, taking a seat next to her husband.

"Nothing much. Just the election." Henry says, quick to send a look towards Gabriel.

"Nothing to worry about, I promise." Gabriel finishes, getting the message loud and clear. Xavier, James, and Ava talk loudly as they come down the stars, Ava jumping down to the ground from the third step.

"See I told you I could do it Uncle James! Didn't I tell him Uncle Xavier?" Ava yells, puffing her chest out because she was proud of her accomplishment. Before long, dinner was served. A wonderful array of fruits, vegetables, and meats were placed on the table.

If you ever walk away from a Collins family meal hungry, it's your own fault. Nobody ended up going to their houses that night. They were too caught up in making sure they all had the same details. Madeline said one thing, Henry another.

Crystal swore by what Henry said, but James did the same by what Madeline had said. Nobody was comfortable with the way Clara had just barged her way into their normally very comfortable lives. Xavier knew his father well enough to know that Clara could very well be his daughter, Crystal was too blind to think her father would ever do something bad, James didn't have enough information to know what to think of the situation, and Gabriel knew for a fact Henry had at least cheated on Madeline, though he was unsure if Clara was his daughter or not.

Crystal and Xavier retreated to their old bedrooms with their husbands, both pairs lost in their own thoughts and wondering if what they had heard could be true or not.

The next morning, everyone gathers in the dining room for breakfast like they hadn't since Crystal moved out.

Adrian had decided to show up during sometime during the night, looking worse than he had in a long time. Breakfast was silent except for forks scraping plates and Ava attempting to talk to everyone around her.

Neither Henry or Madeline went into work that day. They chose to stay home and try to figure out what was going on and what would happen. Henry and Adrian were in the middle of an intense discussion when somebody decided to knock loudly on the door.

"Madeline go get the door." Henry shouted, resuming his conversation with Adrian.

Madeline grumbled to herself, opening the door just as whoever was on the other side of it attempted to knock again.

"Hello, welcome to the Collins fa-" Madeline began, trying to be welcoming even if it was incredibly early.

"We know who you are Mrs. Collins. I'm Detective Lucas Meddia and this is my partner Frank Walters. We've come to ask you some questions about the Seven Hills murders." Lucas at the door says, cutting Madeline off mid-sentence.

The Seven Hills murders were a string of seven murders about nine years prior. The media had called them the "Seven Hills murders" because the number of the victim was cut into each of the victims, and because of each of the victims being found on the top of some nearby hills. The police had never gotten any leads, and had never gotten any substantial evidence.

"Why do you need to question my family? We had nothing to do with those horrible occurrences." Madeline says, her mouth pulling into a frown.

"Mrs. Collins if you and your family could just spare us a few minutes so we can interview you, I promise we will only be here as long as it takes to ask you all a few questions." Frank says, offering up a smile.

"Fine. But when I ask you to leave, you have to leave." Madeline replies, stepping away from the door so the two detectives could pass. Once everyone had gathered in the living room and Ava had been seen off to school, the two detectives started asking questions. They were normal questions that you would think of detectives asking during a murder investigation. They asked about where everyone was, what they were doing at the time, and other such questions.

"We have sat here and answered all of your questions. Please leave now." Henry eventually says, standing up and glaring at the detectives.

"We have things we have to do today". Both of the detectives stood and made their leave, telling the family that they would be back if they had any further inquiries.

CHAPTER 7

Xavier, Please!

When James checks into work the next morning, still preoccupied with what had happened when he was off, he just goes through the motions. James is a reporter, and every morning he works, his assignment is placed on his desk. He had watched people around him move up and get bigger and bigger stories, watched them move on to better and better things, and he was still stuck writing the little articles nobody reads.

Unsurprisingly, there were the little assignments piled up on his desk. James groaned as he sat at his computer chair, reading the basic information for the first article he would have to write today. Without a doubt, he would be able to churn out at least a couple articles before lunch without even having to get up from his chair.

After heading to the break room and getting a cup of the disgusting coffee they serve there, and plugging in some music to listen to as he wrote. At about 10:00 AM James was getting into the swing of things. When he finished the article he was on, he stood and stretched, making his way past his boss's office to the restrooms.

On the way back, James was incredibly surprised to find his boss waiting for him with a smile on his face.

"Come into my office James. We have things to discuss." James' boss, Michael Anders, says, leaving the door to his office open.

James gulps, thinking he did something wrong. He steps into Michael's office, standing nervously as Michael looks at him carefully.

"What do you need sir?" James asks, his hands twitching at his sides as he speaks.

"You are married to Xavier Collins, aren't you?" Michael asks, looking down at a file on his desk.

"You're close with the Collins family then?" He continues when James doesn't answer.

"Yes sir. I am close with the Collins family." James replies, getting over the slight shock he received.

"Good. I want you to report on the murder investigation into the Collins family. It shouldn't be hard for you, all things considering." Michael says, waving his hand dismissively.

James nods his head and walks out the door, a smile making its way onto his face as he sits down again. A couple of his coworkers notice and congratulate him on his "big break" before heading off to do their own projects.

The rest of the day seems to drag on, but James has to finish the rest of the little assignments he was given before he can go and work on the Collins' case. When he finally gets done, which only really takes about an hour or so, James jumps up out of his chair and is through the door before anyone can really react, leaving his cell phone and car keys on his desk in his excitement.

James rushes back into the building, grabs the phone and keys he had left on his desk, and sprints back out the building. He fumbles with his keys for a second before unlocking his car and driving away, headed straight for the apartment he shares with Xavier.

"Xavier! Are you home! I have amazing news!" James shouts, almost tripping on the one step they have in the entire apartment.

"Xavier!" James shouts again, this time listening for the sound of their shower running.

When he hears the faint sound of water hitting the floor, James huffs. Taking a seat at the breakfast bar, he takes a few deep breaths to calm down a bit.

"Come on James, it's not that big of a deal." He says to himself, spinning slightly in the chair.

"That's a lie this is the biggest thing that has ever happened to me!" James groans because of the desire he has to be nonchalant about the whole situation, but the intense need to be over joyous about the occasion. When Xavier finally walks out of the shower, shirtless and rubbing his hair with a towel, James almost jumps out of his skin in his rush to tell Xavier what happened.

"Xavier guess what I did!" James says, just below a shout.

"What did you do Jay?" Xavier asks, noticing right away the excitement that James was displaying.

"I've finally gotten my big break! Mr. Anders asked me to do a huge piece, and I think this is the one thing that will set my career on the fast track to success! This is so big for me!"

James launches into his explanation with full force. Xavier, once he throws a clean shirt on, sits on the couch and motions for James to do the same. Once James complies, Xavier begins to ask him questions about the piece that he would be working on.

As Xavier hears what it is that James has been tasked with his face grows more and more cold. James is lost in his own little world, telling Xavier all about what he has been told to do, not for a second thinking about the repercussions of what the story might do to Gabriel's campaign or the Collins family name.

"What did you do James?" Xavier asks finally, his voice void of any emotion.

James stops in his tracks, actually looking for the first time at his husband's reaction to the news. James gulps.

"How dare you do something so bluntly against this family? I don't like most of them and even I would never have even considered doing this!" Xavier spits, fire in his eyes.

"What about what this little article will do to Gabriel's campaign? What about what this little article will do to the company?" He asks, his voice becoming louder and louder.

James shrinks back into himself, flinching with every harsh word. His confident facade was crumbling before his eyes, as every word Xavier was speaking hit him right where it hurt.

"Xavier please-" James choked out, tears rising in his eyes despite the fact he wanted nothing more than to seem strong.

"No James! You brought this on yourself! You are the one who betrayed the family that has welcomed you with open arms!" Xavier is screaming now, rage in his eyes.

"No Xav-" James starts, cowering before the man he loves.

"Get out of my face James!" Xavier screams, raising his hand like he's going to hit James. James visibly flinches and Xavier laughs, the rage in his heart making him forget all love he holds for James.

Xavier is about to bring his hand down on James' weak and cowering body when somebody knocks on their apartment door.

"Uncle James! Uncle Xavier! Daddy dropped me off!" Ava calls, opening the door and interrupting the scene before her.

"Go to our room James." Xavier says coldly, sending him a look made of pure ice.

James puts his head down and follows the order he was given, tears finally leaking from his eyes. James can't help but fall onto the floor and weep as soon as he steps foot into the bedroom he shares with the man he loves so much.

As he curls into a tighter and tighter ball, James thinks of how, just a short time ago, he was allowed to make a critical decision in their life and marriage for a change. As more tears flow down his face, James lets out a soft sob, thinking of how often this happens, how often Xavier snaps and screams terrible things for no reason.

How often Xavier goes "crazy" for a few hours then comes back, blubbering on about how it will never happen again and how sorry he is for causing James pain. Xavier on the other hand, takes Ava by the hand and tells her softly not to worry about Uncle James.

Xavier, now an expert at making up lies to convince people everything is perfect between himself and James, tells his sweet, innocent niece that "Uncle James just needs to rest for a while" as he leads her out of the apartment. Xavier rests for a second before going out of the door behind Ava, smirking when he hears a light sob come from his room.

As Xavier slams the door he lets his smirk slip into a sweet, innocent smile. Xavier helps Ava up into the booster seat in the back of his car. He laughs like normal when she tells one of the corny jokes 8 year olds learn during school as he buckles her in.

Xavier even listens to Ava as she complains about one of the boys in her class who keeps pulling her hair, completely agreeing with her on the issue, of course.

Ava's innocent giggle and the knowledge of the pain he caused James made Xavier very happy for a few hours. Eventually, Xavier began to feel guilty though, causing him to want to make it up to James in some fashion.

After carefully explaining to Ava that he had done something wrong, Xavier lead her into a shop that sold flowers and picked up a dozen white roses. James had always loved white roses. Xavier seemed preoccupied when he dropped Ava off at her house, smiling and telling her that he and Uncle James would not be going to the family dinner.

"Can't you tell Grandma that for us?" Xavier gave a smile and drove away when Ava said she would do just that.

James lay on the floor for God knows how long, crying until he had no more tears to give. He had believed, really truly believed, that Xavier wouldn't do it again. James told himself that things would be perfectly okay because Xavier had promised it wouldn't happen again.

James wanted nothing more than for Xavier to go back to being the man then he fell in love with, the one who wouldn't hurt a fly. James wanted the man who would hold him and tell him everything would be alright.

Xavier was no longer that man, but James still loved him more than anyone else he knew. When the door to the apartment opened again, James didn't hear it. When the door to their bedroom opened, James flinched a little but had no other reaction.

"James?" Xavier called, his voice soft.

"Could you get up and come to the kitchen please?" Xavier then closed the door to the bedroom to give James time and space. James rouses himself from the stupor of blame and hate he had fallen into. He goes over to the vanity and cleans himself up, making sure to take his time.

Eventually, James opens the door and goes to the kitchen like he was asked. Xavier is seated at the breakfast bar with a bottle of wine and an already almost empty glass. James almost turns and goes back to the bedroom, fully knowing that if Xavier was already almost done with a glass, he would drink the whole bottle.

Instead of running from Xavier, however, James clears his throat and walks the rest of the way into the kitchen. James almost sighs at the sight of Xavier's face. They had almost gotten to six months of no arguments on this scale, and James just knew this fact was weighing on Xavier's shoulders.

He figured that was the reason Xavier was drinking again.

"What do you want Xavier?" James finally asks, averting his eyes when Xavier tries to capture his gaze.

James knows if he lets Xavier's breathtaking almond eyes catch his own he will forgive Xavier in a second, without hesitation.

"Can you forgive me James?" Xavier pulls three white roses from somewhere and presents them to James with a sad smile.

"I know how much you love them." Xavier offers up an empty chuckle and motions to the white roses in his hand.

"I bought the freshest ones I could find." Xavier lays them on the table and pushes them gently towards his husband.

"You promised." James turns away from Xavier as he whispers.

"I know I promised baby. I just don't know how to react in certain situations. I'm so sorry James. I'll try harder next time, I swea-" Xavier is pleading.

"I don't care! You fucking promised me!" James yells, turning back to face Xavier. Xavier stands in shock, noticing the tears in James' eyes.

"James, baby, please let me explain." Xavier reaches for James, his hand falling before he could reach James.

James hangs his head and lets the tears fall, taking a tentative step towards the man he loved so much. Despite the fact Xavier had hurt him so many times before, James still sought out his comfortingly tight grip. James fell into Xavier's arms, instantly feeling better.

Xavier tightened his grip around James, swaying the both of them slightly.

"Promise me you won't hurt me." James mumbles into Xavier's shoulder, lifting his head briefly to look into the eyes of the slightly shorter man.

"I promise. I'll never hurt you again." Xavier says, smiling as tears well up in his eyes.

James sets his head back down on Xavier's shoulder, allowing himself to be swayed from side to side.